FROM MAY'S DIARY

Dear Diary,

Yesterday I was worried because my life seemed boring.

Here's a list of what happened today:

- *My pony, Macaroni, came down with a limp.*
- *He has a corn and can't be ridden for a week or even longer.*
- *I met the biggest snob on earth. Her name is Kimberly.*
- *I'm training Kimberly's pony. His name is Zeus. The only problem is that I don't know how to train ponies.*
- *Corey and Jasmine are doing a craft project. Without me.*
- *They have forgotten I exist.*

I wish my life would go back to being boring.

Other Skylark Books you will enjoy
Ask your bookseller for the books you have missed

BIG RED by Jim Kjelgaard

DON'T EAT THE MYSTERY MEAT!
(Graveyard School #1) by Tom B. Stone

ELVIS IS BACK, AND HE'S IN THE
SIXTH GRADE! by Stephen Mooser

ENCYCLOPEDIA BROWN AND THE CASE OF
THE DEAD EAGLES by Donald J. Sobol

THE GHOST IN THE THIRD ROW
by Bruce Coville

PINHEADS UNITE! (Never Sink Nine #10)
by Gibbs Davis

WHAT IS THE TEACHER'S TOUPEE DOING IN
THE FISH TANK? by Jerry Piasecki

May Rides a New Pony

BONNIE BRYANT

Illustrated by Marcy Ramsey

A SKYLARK BOOK
NEW YORK • TORONTO • LONDON • SYDNEY • AUCKLAND

RL 3,007–10
MAY RIDES A NEW PONY
A Bantam Skylark Book / July 1996

Skylark Books is a registered trademark of Bantam Books, a division of Bantam Doubleday Dell Publishing Group, Inc. Registered in U.S. Patent and Trademark Office and elsewhere. Pony Tails is a registered trademark of Bonnie Bryant Hiller. "USPC" and "Pony Club" are registered trademarks of The United States Pony Clubs, Inc., The Kentucky Horse Park, 4071 Iron Works Pike, Lexington, KY 40511-8462.

ISBN 0-553-48380-3

Published simultaneously in the United States and Canada

Bantam Books are published by Bantam Books, a division of Bantam Doubleday Dell Publishing Group, Inc. Its trademark, consisting of the words "Bantam Books" and the portrayal of a rooster, is Registered in U.S. Patent and Trademark Office and in other countries. Marca Registrada. Bantam Books, 1540 Broadway, New York, New York 10036.

PRINTED IN THE UNITED STATES OF AMERICA

OPM 0 9 8 7 6 5 4 3 2 1

I would like to express my special thanks
to Helen Geraghty for her help
in the writing of this book.

1 What's Wrong with Macaroni?

It was a perfect summer Monday. The Pony Tails were riding their ponies in long, lazy circles around the Grovers' paddock.

"Is this great or what?" said Corey Takamura.

"Great," said Jasmine James.

"Miserable!" said May Grover.

Jasmine and Corey turned to look at May in wonder.

"What's wrong?" Corey asked.

May took a deep breath. A week earlier, she'd gotten a diary for her birthday. And not a single exciting thing had happened since.

May knew that a diary was just a bunch of blank pages. She knew her diary wasn't human. But somehow that didn't matter. She was beginning to get the feeling that her diary thought she was boring.

"What am I going to put in my diary?" she asked the others.

"You could explain about the Pony Tails," said Corey. "How we're totally pony-crazy. And how we're not a club but just good friends."

"I did that on Friday," May groaned.

"You could tell how Corey moved into the house between your house and my house," Jasmine said.

"I did that on Saturday," May moaned. "I've told everything there is to tell."

From inside the Grovers' barn came a thumping sound.

"What's that?" Jasmine asked. "That could be interesting."

"Dad's getting a new horse. He's fixing the stall," May said. Mr. Grover was a horse trainer, and he was always having horses stay over in the stable.

"Every day doesn't have to be exciting," said Jasmine.

"That's easy for you to say," May grumbled. "You don't have a diary."

May Rides a New Pony

Macaroni, May's pony, snorted and tossed his yellow mane.

"Did you see that?" May wailed. "Even Macaroni thinks I'm boring."

Corey and Jasmine exchanged worried looks. May was really upset.

Macaroni stumbled.

"Wait a second," Corey said. "I don't think Macaroni is bored. I think it's something else."

Macaroni moved forward in a slow, lurching walk.

"What's wrong, Mac?" said May.

"I think it's his right front foot," Corey said. Corey's mom, who was known as Doc Tock, was a veterinarian. She didn't take care of horses—she took care of small animals. But Corey had learned a lot from her.

Suddenly May was all business. If there was something wrong with Macaroni's foot, she knew she had to find out what it was right away.

Gently she steered Macaroni over to the fence and got ready to dismount. She kicked both her feet out of the stirrups and put her left hand on Macaroni's neck and her right hand on the pommel of his saddle. She swung her right leg over the saddle and jumped down.

She went around to his other side to look at his right foot. Macaroni was holding it cocked forward so that only the front rim of his hoof was touching the ground.

Macaroni wouldn't do that unless his foot hurt.

May led Macaroni to the side of the ring.

Just then Mr. Grover appeared at the door of the barn. "What's up?" he asked when he saw May looking at Macaroni's hoof.

"Mac has a sore foot."

Mr. Grover nodded. "Do you need help?"

May was glad her father was there in case she needed him. But she wanted to handle this herself. "It's probably a stone," she said. "I'll get the hoof pick and clean out his hoof."

"Good idea," Mr. Grover said.

May led Macaroni into the barn and put him in his stall. She took off his saddle and bridle and put on his halter. Then she fastened a rope to one side of his halter and another rope to the other side. She tied each

one to the sides of the stall. She was being extracareful.

She went to the tack room and got the hoof pick.

When she came back, she showed it to Mac. "It's just a pick," she said. "I'm going to be supergentle."

Macaroni nodded as if he understood.

May put her right hand on Macaroni's neck and ran it slowly down to his chest, then to his leg, and finally down to his knee. Macaroni raised his foot.

May propped his hoof against her leg and looked at it. The inside of the shoe was caked with dirt.

"This won't hurt," she said.

I hope, she thought.

Being very careful, she inserted the hoof pick under the edge of the clod of dirt. She pried, but nothing happened. The dirt was firmly stuck. She pried a little harder. One edge of the clod came away. Gently she lifted it off.

She turned the clod over. All she could see was dirt. But a stone could be hidden inside. She crumbled it.

There was no stone.

She looked at Macaroni's hoof. Something must be wrong with it. Softly she touched it.

Macaroni jumped. He jerked his foot away. His coat twitched. His ears went back. For a second May was afraid he was going to rear onto his hind legs. But then he sighed, as if he were sighing the pain out of his body. He shook himself, sending his yellow forelock into his eyes.

May knew she needed to tell her father about this.

She walked to the end of the stall and called, "Dad?"

Mr. Grover appeared almost instantly.

"It's not a stone. It's something else," May said. "When I touched the inside of Mac's hoof, it was really sore."

Mr. Grover nodded. "What do you think you should do?" It was one of the rules of the Grovers' stable that May was in charge of Macaroni.

"I guess I'd better call Judy Barker," she said. Judy Barker was a horse vet in Willow Creek, the town in Virginia where the Pony Tails lived.

"Good thinking," Mr. Grover said.

* * *

An hour later May felt a lot better. Judy Barker had come and examined Macaroni and said that it was nothing serious, just a corn.

"Great," May said. "Er . . . what's a corn?"

"A corn is like the calluses that grow on people's feet," said Judy. "It has a virus inside."

To May this sounded totally creepy. "Is there a cure?" she said.

"All you have to do is call the blacksmith," Judy said. "He'll come and take it out."

"Will it hurt?" May said.

"A little." Judy nodded. "But Macaroni will be glad to be rid of that corn. And, knowing Macaroni the way I do, I'm sure he'll handle the whole thing well."

"That's Mac," May said proudly. Macaroni was famous for his calm, friendly nature. At Pine Hollow Stables, where she, Corey, and Jasmine took riding lessons, Macaroni was known as the smartest, sweetest, and friendliest pony. In fact, since Macaroni was the color of macaroni and cheese, and since he was totally cool, his nickname was Mellow Yellow.

"After the blacksmith takes the corn out, he'll fit Macaroni with a special shoe," Judy said. "The shoe will protect the sore spot where the corn used to be."

"So that's it," said May happily. "Everything will be fine."

"Absolutely," Judy said. "Of course you won't be able to ride Macaroni for a week or two."

"A week or two?" May said.

"He'll sleep a lot," Judy said. "He won't even miss riding."

"Hey, that's . . . great," May said. She walked with Judy to the blue pickup truck and waved good-bye as Judy drove away.

Corey and Jasmine ran over to May.

"What's the story?" Jasmine asked.

"It's a corn," May said. "No big deal. The blacksmith will come and take it out in the morning."

"That's great," Corey said.

"Yeah, I guess," May said.

"What's wrong?" Jasmine said.

"I can't go riding for a week," May said. "Or two." She shook her head. "Why did I wish something exciting would happen?"

2 The Craft Fair

"Just because Macaroni has to rest doesn't mean *you* can't ride," Jasmine said. "You can ride Outlaw."

Outlaw was Jasmine's pony. He had a white mask that looked like an outlaw's mask, and a brown coat and mane. Not only was he called Outlaw, he *was* an outlaw. When Jasmine told him to trot, he wanted to canter. When she wanted him to canter, he wanted to gallop.

May knew that riding Outlaw would be a challenge.

"That's really nice of you," she said. "I totally appreciate it."

"You can also ride Sam," Corey said. Sam had a curved white blaze like a samurai sword on his nose. Sam was as bold and independent as a samurai warrior.

May knew she would have fun riding Sam.

"Thanks," she said. "That's really great. The only thing is"—she took a deep breath—"I already miss riding Macaroni."

"I know how you feel," Corey said. "If it was Sam, I'd feel the same way." She put her arms around May.

"Me too," said Jasmine, putting her arms around the two of them.

"Poor May," Corey said. "We've got to do something."

"Wait a second. I have an idea," Jasmine said. "How about some homemade cookies and a glass of milk?" Jasmine knew May was crazy about her mother's cookies.

May felt a bit better. Not only was Jasmine's mother an artist at painting and crafts, she was an artist at baking. May thought Mrs. James's cookies belonged in the Cookie Hall of Fame.

"I guess I could handle it," May said, grinning.

As they headed for Jasmine's house, they walked through May's backyard and then through Corey's.

"We're Pony Tails on the Pony Trail," May said cheerfully. "We've worn our own special trail through the three backyards." She pointed to the faint but unmistakable path leading from one backyard to another.

"I like it," Corey said. "Pony Tails on the Pony Trail heading for a supersnack."

The trail led straight to Jasmine's back door.

Jasmine opened the door and let them into the mudroom, where the James family kept boots and other messy things. The Pony Tails took off their boots and hung them upside down on the boot rack. Jasmine put on the sneakers she'd left next to the door. May and Corey put on the special felt slippers that Mrs. James had made for guests.

They walked into the kitchen.

Mrs. James was sitting at the table.

"Hi, Mrs. J.," said May. May had known Mrs. James forever. In fact, she had known her more than forever. May's mom and Mrs. James had been friends when they were pregnant with May and Jasmine.

"Hi," said Mrs. James without much enthusiasm.

May Rides a New Pony

It wasn't like Mrs. James to give May such a small hello. May wondered if something was wrong.

Jasmine lifted the lid off the cookie jar and said, "We've got chocolate chip cookies. We've got oatmeal. We've got peanut butter. We've got pecan."

"Oh dear," said Mrs. James.

"Is something wrong?" Jasmine said.

"It's that horrible cookie smell," Mrs. James said.

May, Corey, and Jasmine looked at each other in amazement. How could the smell of freshly baked cookies be horrible?

"What is it, Mom?" Jasmine said.

"It's morning sickness," said Mrs. James, putting her hand on her stomach.

"Mornings make you sick?" said May.

"It's because I'm pregnant," Mrs. James explained. "The first thing in the morning I feel kind of . . ."

"Yucky?" May said.

"That's just the word I was searching for," Mrs. James said with a wan smile. "I feel better as the day wears on."

"When you were pregnant with me, did I make you sick?" asked Jasmine.

"It's part of being pregnant," Mrs. James said.

"That's terrible," Jasmine said. "I'm really sorry."

"Believe me, it was worth it," Mrs. James said. "I have you."

But she still looked miserable.

Jasmine put her arms around her mom's shoulders and said, "What's wrong?"

With their long hair and their delicate faces, Mrs. James and Jasmine looked a lot alike, May thought.

"I signed up for the craft fair at your school before I knew I was pregnant. And it's on Friday," Mrs. James said. "And I've been so tired I've hardly done anything."

May knew that Mrs. James was great at arts and crafts. But if Mrs. James felt sick because she was pregnant, May was sure the school would understand.

"Just tell them," she said.

"I hate to let them down," Mrs. James said. "They're raising money for the library."

"Wait a second," May said to Corey and Jasmine. "I think this calls for a meeting of the Pony Tails." She turned to Mrs. James.

"If there's one thing the Pony Tails are good at, it's—"

"—solving problems," said May, Corey, and Jasmine at the same time.

When the Pony Tails said the same thing at the same time, they always gave each other the Pony Tail salute—they slapped each other high fives and said "Jake." In Pony Tail lingo, *jake* meant great.

"This is a pretty big problem," Mrs. James said.

"No problem is too big for the Pony Tails," May said. She motioned Corey and Jasmine over to a spot next to the refrigerator.

"So what do we do?" Jasmine said.

"Er," May said, "there's bound to be a terrific solution. I know there is. I'm totally sure."

She tried to look as if she were about to come up with a great idea. But her mind was blank.

"Wait a second," Corey said. "We can . . ." She paused dramatically.

May and Jasmine leaned closer.

"We can make craft items *for* her," Corey said.

"Great idea," Jasmine said. "I know how to use the sewing machine."

Terrible idea, May thought. If there was one thing May was bad at, it was sewing.

"I can't run the sewing machine," Corey said. "But I can sew by hand."

They looked at May.

"Um," she said.

Jasmine and Corey ran over to Mrs. James.

"Can we help?" Jasmine said. "We can make craft items."

"Could you?" said Mrs. James, smiling hopefully. "That would be wonderful."

"We'll be neat," Corey said.

May could see that the situation was getting out of hand. No way was she going to spend the entire week sewing. "We can do *some* sewing," she said, "but don't forget we were going to go swimming. And pick blackberries."

"That can wait," Jasmine said.

May was stunned. How could swimming wait? How could picking blackberries wait?

"What should we make?" Corey said.

"I've got a craft book upstairs," Jasmine said. "It's crammed with ideas."

May Rides a New Pony

Jasmine and Corey headed toward the stairs.

May watched them. Were they crazy? Were they planning to spend this beautiful day inside?

"I guess I better check on Macaroni," she said in a loud voice. "I guess Macaroni is wondering where I am."

"Say hi to him," said Jasmine over her shoulder.

"Give him a big hug," said Corey.

As if they care, May thought. The only thing they can think about is their project.

Jasmine and Corey disappeared at the top of the stairs.

"See you," said May softly.

She jammed her hands into her pockets and turned toward the door.

"Is everything all right?" asked Mrs. James.

"Sure," May said. "Absolutely. Completely."

"Would you like to take Macaroni an apple?" Mrs. James asked. She pointed to the bowl of apples in the center of the kitchen table.

They were tiny red-and-green apples, Macaroni's favorite.

"Thanks, Mrs. J.," May said.

"Take two," Mrs. James said. "They're small."

May nodded. She took another apple, popped one into each pocket, and headed toward the door.

She could tell Macaroni about how her friends were ignoring her because of the craft project, she thought. He would understand.

3 The Idea

May stuck her head into Macaroni's stall. "Hi, Mac. I've got a couple of apples for you."

He turned, blinking heavily, and yawned.

Great, May thought, he's supposed to be resting and I woke him up.

"Go back to sleep, Mac," she said.

His head bobbed. His eyelids went down. May heard a faint snorty sound. Macaroni was snoring.

She wandered into the tack room, where her dad was cleaning a saddle.

"Hi, May, what's up?" Mr. Grover asked.

"Nothing," May said.

"Where are Corey and Jasmine?"

"They're doing a craft project," May said

glumly. "It's sewing. You know me. When I sew, people laugh."

"No one's good at everything," Mr. Grover said.

"You're telling me," said May miserably.

Mr. Grover eyed her curiously. "How long is this sewing project going to last?"

"Forever," May said. But then she could see her dad waiting for her to be more precise. "Until Friday."

"This is Monday. It's going to last until Friday," Mr. Grover said. "That's a long time."

"*Long* is putting it mildly," May said.

Mr. Grover finished polishing the saddle and put the chamois cloth back into the plastic carrier that held the polishing supplies. He lifted the saddle back onto the rack.

"Why don't you come and get the new horse with me?" he asked. "It will give you something to do."

May thought about it. She didn't want Corey and Jasmine to see her moping around the barn. And anyway, meeting a new horse would be interesting.

"Thanks, Dad," she said.

May Rides a New Pony

As they headed out of the barn, Mr. Grover said, "You're not going to believe what this horse is called."

"What?"

"Zeus. Isn't that strange?"

"Totally strange," said May as she walked with her dad toward the family station wagon. "Um . . . why is it strange?"

"Zeus was the king of the gods in ancient Greece," Mr. Grover said.

"Well, it must be some horse," May said.

"My thoughts exactly," said Mr. Grover with a smile.

* * *

Corey and Jasmine were lying on Jasmine's bed staring glumly at the craft book.

"I thought for sure this book would be full of ideas," Jasmine said. "And it is full of ideas, but . . ."

"But none of them are right," Corey said.

Jasmine nodded. She wanted their project to be outstanding. After all, the other craft items at the fair would be made by adults.

"What we need is a really brilliant idea," Corey said.

"And that's exactly what we haven't got," said Jasmine.

"If May were here, she'd have one," Corey said. "She always has good ideas."

"But she's worried about Macaroni," Jasmine said. "She wants to be with him."

"That makes sense," Corey said.

Corey turned to a page that was filled with pictures of pillows. "We could make pillows."

"Too boring," Jasmine said.

Corey turned the page. The next page was filled with pictures of teddy bears.

"We could make bears," Jasmine said.

"Too hard," Corey said. She pointed to a pattern for a bear. "That one needs twelve pieces. We'd be lucky to make one bear by Friday."

"I think we're stuck," Jasmine said.

"Why don't we go ask your mom?" Corey said.

"Hey." Jasmine giggled. "Why didn't I think of that?"

They walked downstairs and into the kitchen.

Mrs. James was sitting at the table sewing red and yellow pieces of material together.

"What's that?" Corey asked.

"It's a tea cozy," said Mrs. James. "When you put it over a teapot, it keeps the tea warm."

"Great idea," Corey said. Then she remembered that she and Jasmine had no ideas at all. "We're totally stuck."

"You couldn't find anything in the book?" asked Mrs. James.

"Pillows are too boring, and bears are too hard," Corey said.

"Hmmm," said Mrs. James. "Maybe I can help." She put down the tea cozy and frowned. She looked up at the ceiling, then down at the table. "Ah," she said. "Why don't you make pony pillows?"

"Ponies don't need pillows," Corey said. "They sleep on straw."

"I mean pillows shaped like ponies," Mrs. James said. "You can cut pony shapes out of fabric, sew them, and stuff them. Willow Creek is full of pony lovers. I think pony pillows might be popular."

"Good idea," Corey said.

Jasmine smiled. She had known her mom would come up with a great idea.

"But how?" Corey asked. "It sounds hard."

"It's not as hard as it sounds," Mrs. James

said. She went over to a drawer next to the telephone and pulled out a sheet of paper and a pencil. She brought them back to the table.

"I hear you're good at drawing ponies," she said to Corey.

"She's great," Jasmine said. "She draws the best ponies ever."

Corey had been drawing ponies half her life, but suddenly she felt nervous. What if she drew a terrible pony?

"You can do it," Jasmine said.

Corey hunched over the sheet of paper. She started with the pony's ears. She knew that was an odd place to start, but that was the way she always drew ponies. She made one ear a little forward and the other one back. Then she drew the upward curve of the pony's neck and the downward curve of the pony's back. She raised the line in another curve for the pony's rump. She drew the tail, making it long and wispy. She did the two backward Cs of the hind legs. And two neat hooves.

The pencil flew across the paper. There were the pony's stomach, his front legs, and then his head.

Corey sat back. Sometimes her ponies came out really odd-looking. But this pony was okay.

"That's the best pony I ever saw," Jasmine said.

"It's really excellent," said Mrs. James. "Now draw a line half an inch outside the outline of the pony."

Corey did that.

Mrs. James handed her a pair of scissors. "Cut along that line."

Corey did.

"Now you have a pony pillow pattern," Mrs. James said. "Pin that to cloth and cut around it."

"Wow," Corey said. "These pony pillows are going to be the best pony pillows ever made." She giggled. "They may also be the only pony pillows ever made."

Corey turned to Jasmine, expecting her to look happy. But Jasmine had on a worried frown.

"I just remembered something," she said. "May hates to sew."

"Not pony pillows," Corey said. "She'll love sewing them."

"I don't know," Jasmine said. She kept remembering how everyone had teased May about her sewing at camp the summer before.

"We'll talk her into it," Corey said. "She's going to wind up as pony-pillow-crazy as we are."

"Come into the sewing room," Mrs. James said. "I'll give you my bag of fabric scraps. You can choose anything you want."

The three of them walked into the sewing room, which was just off the kitchen. Mrs. James picked up a blue denim laundry bag and handed it to Jasmine.

Jasmine upended it, pouring fabric scraps onto the floor.

"There are so many of them," Corey said. "They're so beautiful. How will we ever choose?"

4 Meeting Zeus

"What if Zeus doesn't fit in the trailer?" said May. "If he's king of the gods, he's bound to be pretty large."

"He'll fit," Mr. Grover said. "The trailer stalls are bigger than you think."

They climbed into the front of the Grovers' beat-up old station wagon. As Mr. Grover turned the key, the engine started with a cough. He put his foot on the gas pedal, and the wagon and horse trailer rattled down the driveway.

Mr. Grover turned left onto the paved county road and drove for several minutes. Then he turned left again and pulled into the driveway of a large brick house with green shutters and huge chimneys at either end. Everything about the house was so new and tidy that it looked unreal.

"That's some house," said May. The Grovers' house was nice, but it had a lived-in look.

"The Randalls just moved in," Mr. Grover said. "From what I hear, they've only been here a few weeks. Everything is new for them, including Zeus."

The Grovers' station wagon and horse trailer clanked up the driveway, past the house and to the barn. Mr. Grover climbed out, stretching his arms.

An amazing sight appeared from a side door of the house. Standing on the doorstep was a girl about May's age. She was wearing pleated linen pants, a silk blouse, and a gold belt. May looked down at her own outfit, which consisted of jeans, a pair of dusty old boots, and a T-shirt that said MARVIN'S CAR REPAIR.

"Are you the horse people?" asked the girl as she took in May's outfit. She didn't sneer, but she didn't have to. Her opinion of May's clothes was obvious.

"That's us, half-horse, half-human," said

Marvin's
CAR
Repair

May jokingly. She brushed her uncombed brown hair out of her eyes.

Mr. Grover nudged her. May remembered that training horses was a business for him, and he had to be polite to his customers, no matter how obnoxious they might be.

"I guess you just moved in," said May, trying to be friendly.

"I'll be leaving for sleepaway camp tomorrow," the girl said. "I'll be gone for a month."

May understood she was supposed to be impressed. But personally, she had no desire to go to sleepaway camp. Things were too much fun in Willow Creek.

A man in a blue business suit came out the door behind the girl. "You must be Mr. Grover," he said, striding toward them. "I see you've met Kimberly."

"That's right," Mr. Grover said, "and this is my daughter May."

Kimberly gave May a snooty look.

"Have you met Zeus?" Mr. Randall asked.

"Not yet," Mr. Grover said. "But I'm looking forward to it."

"Come on." Mr. Randall walked to the stable and threw open the barn door.

The barn was one of the fanciest May had ever seen. There were four stalls, each with an elaborate wooden door and a brass nameplate.

Only one plate had a name on it. The name was Zeus. The only problem was that Zeus seemed to be invisible. May couldn't see any horse in the stall.

Mr. Randall opened the stall door. Inside was a brown pony. A *small* brown pony. If Mr. Grover sat on the pony his feet would touch the ground.

"Ah," Mr. Grover said. "Yes, ummm." He looked totally stumped. May knew that the only way to train a pony was by riding it. But there was no way Mr. Grover could ride this pony.

"How come you called him Zeus?" May asked.

Mr. Randall smiled. "Kimberly is a great student. What she doesn't know about Greek mythology isn't worth knowing. We always call her Princess. So she thought she might as well name her horse after the king of the gods."

Mr. Grover looked at May. His eyes were moist. May could tell he was struggling to keep from laughing. May had to look at the ground to keep from laughing herself.

"We have a problem here," said Mr. Grover solemnly. "I was expecting a horse."

"Horse, pony, what's the difference?" Mr. Randall asked.

May wondered what her dad was going to do. Horse trainers had a lot of expenses, and the Grovers weren't rich. In fact, the family always joked that being only somewhat poor was their dream. Mr. Grover couldn't afford to turn the job down, but he couldn't do it properly, either.

"I can't ride Zeus," Mr. Grover said.

"But you have an assistant who can," May said.

Mr. Grover looked at her curiously.

May knew she had to do this right. Otherwise no one would believe her.

"What I don't know about ponies isn't worth knowing," she said. "I've ridden them, trained them, and showed them. Other pony trainers ask me for advice."

Mr. Grover's face was now bright red. May couldn't tell whether he was angry or amused.

Kimberly looked at May's outfit. "You're a

pony trainer?" She obviously didn't believe a word May had said.

"We pony trainers don't like to dress up," May said. "It's a matter of style."

Kimberly stared at May's MARVIN'S CAR REPAIR T-shirt. "That's style?"

May knew she had to act fast. She walked into Zeus's stall. Luckily, she still had the apples she'd meant to give Macaroni. She put one on the flat palm of her hand and let Zeus sniff it.

Zeus neatly grabbed the apple with his teeth. He chewed it, swallowed it, and looked at her as if he was waiting for something else. Suddenly he leaned forward and gently nipped at the pocket that held the other apple.

"How did you know I had another?" May asked. "You're one smart pony." She gave him the other apple.

Zeus had bright, lively eyes and a long brown mane and forelock. He might be small, but he was a great-looking pony.

"I think we're going to get along," May said to him.

Then she realized that the others were waiting for her. She walked out and closed the stall door behind her.

"No problem," she said. "I can see Zeus is inexperienced, but he has a good attitude, and he's intelligent. I don't think there will be any trouble. You'll be amazed at what I can do with Zeus in a month."

"But you're so . . . young," Mr. Randall said.

"Young, but very experienced," May said.

Mr. Grover, who was standing behind Mr. Randall, rolled his eyes and looked at the sky.

"If you can give me a couple of hours, I'll explain what I'm planning to do," May said. "My pony training ideas are complex, but I think you'll find them interesting. For instance . . ." She clasped her hands and tried to look as if she were about to give a long, boring speech.

Hurriedly Mr. Randall looked at his watch. "I've got to get back to work." He turned to his daughter. "How about you, Kimberly?"

"I've got to pack for camp," she said. "The maid never does it right. I've got to do it myself."

"That's tough," May said. "But I can loan you a book that explains my training techniques. It's a really thick book. If you read it every night after dinner, you can finish by the end of camp."

"Never mind," Kimberly said airily. "I think I have something better to do with my evenings."

May heaved a sigh of relief.

Then Mr. Randall's beeper went off. He grabbed it from his pocket and read the message. "Sorry," he said, "something has come up." He looked from May to Mr. Grover. "So everything's settled?"

"Definitely," May said. "Zeus is in good hands."

The Randalls disappeared into their house.

"I didn't know you were a pony trainer," Mr. Grover said. He was trying to look stern, but his eyes were twinkling.

"It's a surprise I was saving for you," May said.

"*Surprise* is the right word," Mr. Grover said. "So, Ms. Pony Trainer, what do we do now?"

May rubbed her chin thoughtfully. "I would say the first step is to get Zeus home."

Mr. Grover grinned. "Good thinking."

A horrible thought crossed May's mind. What if Zeus was trailer-shy? A lot of ponies really hated horse trailers. If May couldn't get Zeus into the trailer, it would look bad.

She glanced at the Randalls' house. Kimberly was standing at an upstairs window, watching.

"Do you want me to help?" Mr. Grover asked.

"No," May said. "I can do this myself."

Maybe, she thought. Or maybe this is going to be one big disaster.

Casually she walked into Zeus's stall.

"You're about to have a really fun experience," she said to Zeus. Then she realized that sounded phony, so she started again. "You're about to go in a trailer. You might not like trailers. You might really hate trailers. But at the other end of your ride is going to be the greatest stable on earth. Namely the Grover stable."

Zeus looked at her with bright, expectant eyes.

"Please help," she said.

Zeus nodded and looked friendly.

"Here goes," she said. She clipped the

lead rope onto his halter and led him out of the stall.

Outside, she saw that Mr. Grover had let down the trailer ramp.

"So here we go," she said to Zeus.

She took a step onto the ramp. It clanked. Oh well, she thought, here goes nothing. He's never going to follow me.

Zeus trotted up the ramp, his hooves making neat clicking sounds. May stood to the side so that he could enter the stall. This was the tough part. Lots of ponies would go to the top of the ramp but then change their minds about walking into the narrow stall.

"There you go," she said.

Zeus moved past her into the stall. She closed the door.

"You are the world's greatest pony," she said to Zeus's rump.

Zeus nickered as if he agreed.

When May climbed into the front seat of the Grovers' station wagon, Mr. Grover said, "Nice work, May."

"I think Zeus might be the greatest pony on earth," she said. "With the exception of Macaroni, that is."

The station wagon with the horse trailer

behind it clanked past the Randalls' house. Looking up, May saw that Kimberly was still watching from the window. May tossed her a casual wave.

As they turned out onto the paved road, Mr. Grover said, "Thanks, May."

"For what?" she asked.

"I was kind of in a hole," he said. "You got me out."

"Hey," she said, "we trainers have got to stick together."

"True," Mr. Grover said. He was grinning from ear to ear.

When they got to the Grovers' stable, May backed Zeus out of the horse trailer. Although most ponies hated walking backward, Zeus was cheerful and frisky. When they got to the bottom, May led him into the stall her dad had prepared.

"You're going to like it here," she said to Zeus. "And I'm going to love you." She put her arms around his neck and felt the slow, easy rhythm of his breathing. "And you're going to love Macaroni. I know the two of you will be best friends."

When May had Zeus settled, she went to the feed room to get a carrot for Macaroni.

Macaroni was awake now. He was munching on hay and looking like his usual mellow self.

"I've got great news," May said. "We have a new pony for a while. His name is Zeus."

Macaroni grabbed the carrot she held out and chomped it to bits.

"Zeus is smart," May said. She was about to tell Macaroni how Zeus had found the apple in her pocket, when Macaroni yawned.

"Okay, so you're still sleepy," May said.

She went off to look for Corey and Jasmine.

She knocked on the back door of the Jameses' house.

Mrs. James came out. "Hi, May. Corey and Jasmine just went to the shopping center."

"Oh," May said. Corey and Jasmine knew she loved going to the shopping center. Why hadn't they asked her?

"How come they didn't tell me?" May asked.

"It was an emergency," Mrs. Grover said. "They needed notions right away."

May was totally confused. "What's a notion?"

"Buttons and thread and yarn," Mrs. James said. "They need them for the pony pillows."

"Pony pillows?"

"Their project for the craft fair."

"Oh, right," May said. She was trying to pretend that she knew all about the project. But she didn't know anything about it.

Mrs. James must have noticed that something was bothering May because she asked, "Is anything wrong?"

"Nothing at all," May said. "Everything is totally great. I've got this new pony I'm training. How could anything be better?"

"I'll tell Jasmine and Corey you were here," Mrs. James said. "I know they'll be excited to hear that you're training a new pony. I'm sure they'll go over to your house to meet him."

But Jasmine and Corey never came.

That night May wrote in her diary:

Dear Diary,

Yesterday I was worried because my life seemed boring.

Here's a list of what happened today:

Macaroni came down with a limp.

He has a corn and can't be ridden for a week or even longer.

I met the biggest snob on earth. Her name is Kimberly.

I'm training Kimberly's pony. His name is Zeus. The only problem is that I don't know how to train ponies.

Corey and Jasmine are doing a craft project. Without me.

They have forgotten I exist.

I wish my life would go back to being boring.

5 Training with Dad

It was barely light when May opened her eyes. Usually when she woke this early, she rolled over and went back to sleep. But Zeus was in the barn. There was pony training to do.

She got dressed and went down to the kitchen, where she filled a bowl with cereal and poured herself a glass of milk.

Mr. Grover ambled into the kitchen, yawning and rubbing his eyes.

"May," he said, "what are you doing up at this hour?"

"A pony trainer has to get up bright and early," May said.

Mr. Grover looked at his watch. "I like your attitude," he said. He walked over to the toaster and popped in an English muffin. Then he turned on the coffee machine. The machine sputtered, and in a few minutes the kitchen smelled of fresh coffee.

"So where do we start?" May said.

"We have to find out how much Zeus knows," Mr. Grover said. "We'll have to start with the longe line."

May had been looking forward to riding Zeus, but she knew her father was right. They had to start slow and easy.

"I never handled a horse on a line," she said.

"It's easy," Mr. Grover said. "You'll be good at it."

May waited while her father drank his coffee and ate his English muffin. Finally he said, "Let's go."

They walked out to the barn and into the tack room.

"I guess we need the cavesson," May said. That was a special halter with a metal ring in the center of the strap that went across the pony's nose.

"That's right," said Mr. Grover.

"And the longe line," May said. That was a long leather strap that was attached to the ring on the cavesson.

"And the whip, and the gloves." May picked them up. She knew that if she didn't wear gloves, the line would hurt her hands. And if she didn't have a whip, Zeus wouldn't know when to move.

"All set," she said.

"One more thing," Mr. Grover said. "A riding hat."

"But I won't be riding Zeus."

"When you're working with a new horse, you should always wear a hat because you can't tell what's going to happen," said Mr. Grover.

May got her black riding hat and put it on.

She went into Zeus's stall and showed him the cavesson, the line, and the whip. "I know this seems like a lot of equipment," she said to him, "but this is what we'll be using."

Zeus seemed curious.

May took off his halter and put on the cavesson. Then she snapped the line onto the cavesson ring. She led Zeus out of his stall and into the ring.

Mr. Grover was leaning on the fence, waiting.

"Give him about twelve feet of line," he said.

May unlooped the line from her left hand.

"Ask him to walk," Mr. Grover said.

May shook the line.

Zeus looked at her with interest, but he didn't move.

She realized it was time to use the whip. She gave Zeus a small tap on his rear.

He started to walk.

"So far so good," she said to her dad.

After Zeus had walked around the ring twice, Mr. Grover said, "How about a trot?"

She tapped Zeus on the rear. He burst into a snappy trot, lifting his knees high.

"Nice trot," Mr. Grover said. "This is a pony with talent."

May felt proud for Zeus. "I knew you were great," she said to him.

"He's been ridden by someone who knows and cares about ponies," Mr. Grover said. He smiled at May. "Just like you."

A few minutes later Jasmine and Corey appeared on the other side of the fence. They climbed up and leaned over the top.

"You're training a pony," Jasmine said.

"I'm just a beginner," May said modestly. "But it's really interesting."

"How do you know what to do?" Corey asked.

"My dad tells me." May was about to launch into a speech about how important it was to wear a hat when you were working with a new pony. But then she noticed that Corey and Jasmine weren't paying attention.

"Purple eyes don't go with a green mane," Corey said.

"They do!" Jasmine said.

"Purple eyes with a pink mane would be much better," Corey said.

"They would not!" Jasmine said. "I can't believe you said that."

"I'll show you." Corey climbed off the fence. Jasmine climbed down after her. They headed toward the Jameses' house.

Well, May thought, at least I can be a good pony trainer. She turned back to Zeus. "Okay," she said, "let's work on that trot. I want to see high knees."

Half an hour later May noticed that Mr. Grover was watching from the outside of the ring.

"You and Zeus are doing so well, I think it's time to saddle up," he said.

"For real?" May said. The truth was that her left arm was getting tired, and she was getting dizzy from watching Zeus move in circles around the ring. "Like right now?"

"Right now," Mr. Grover said with a smile.

May led Zeus back to his stall.

She got the bridle and saddle Mr. Grover had brought over from the Randalls' stable. Naturally, they were new and expensive. But Zeus deserved them.

When May put the bridle and saddle on him, Zeus frisked in his stall, ready to go.

She led him outside, mounted, and walked him twice around the paddock. Zeus was already warm from his work on the longe line, but May didn't want him to get the idea that he could go straight into a trot.

After Zeus had walked around the paddock twice more, May pressed her knees against his sides and loosened the reins. Zeus broke into a light, airy trot. It felt wonderful and exciting.

Macaroni's trot was solid and comfortable. Macaroni was totally surefooted. She could trot him anywhere and not worry that he would fall.

Her first pony, Luna, had a slow, rocking trot. Riding Luna had been like sitting in a swing.

All ponies have different gaits, May thought. And Zeus's are wonderful!

* * *

Corey sat on the floor cutting out ponies. Jasmine was at the sewing machine sewing them together.

At first Corey had had trouble following the pattern, but she had gotten better. In fact, now she was having fun. Mrs. James's scissors were sharp. If Corey held them right, they seemed to fly through the fabric.

"I think we're actually going to be able to make these pony pillows after all," Jasmine said.

"At first I wasn't sure," said Corey. "But now I think you're right."

Corey finished the pony shapes she'd been cutting and carried them over to Jasmine at the machine. She went back to the heap of fabric to look for another big scrap.

Corey picked up a checkered print with

cutouts of ponies sewn to it. She touched one of the ponies and saw that it was sewn to the fabric by hand.

"Will you look at this?" Corey said.

Jasmine rubbed her eyes. "Sewing can really make you cross-eyed," she said. She looked at the piece of fabric.

"That's my old dress," she said. "My mother made it for my sixth birthday."

"It's beautiful," Corey said.

"When I outgrew that dress I thought I was going to cry," Jasmine said. "I loved that dress."

"Don't worry," Corey said. "It will make the best pony pillow ever."

6 Zeus the Wonder Pony

Two days later May couldn't believe the progress Zeus had made. To get him to trot, all she had to do was close her legs around his belly and slightly loosen the reins. The minute she did, Zeus pranced forward. When she wanted him to stop, all she had to do was to press down firmly through her seat and pull lightly on the reins.

This did not mean that Zeus was perfect. He was a young pony, after all. Sometimes he didn't obey her. Once he trotted sideways across the ring. But it was clear that he wanted to learn.

"Zeus has a natural talent for learning," May said to her father. "I can't believe how smart he is."

"You have a natural talent for training,"

Mr. Grover said. "You've done wonders with him."

May wished she could tell Corey and Jasmine about the training. But they didn't seem interested.

They had promised to take her mind off Macaroni's sore foot. Instead, they were ignoring her. On Wednesday, during their riding lesson at Pine Hollow, all they'd been able to talk about was sewing.

May had been planning to go to the craft fair on Friday with them, but now she wasn't even sure she was invited.

She was thinking about the fair as she led Zeus into the barn. Suddenly she heard a very lonely whinny from Macaroni's stall. She saw him peering out at her.

Talk about being ignored! May realized she'd spent hardly any time with Macaroni since Zeus had arrived.

As soon as Zeus was settled in his stall, May went back to see Macaroni.

"How's your foot?" she asked.

Macaroni raised his foot as if he'd been dying for her to ask. It looked much better since the blacksmith had removed the corn two days earlier, but it was still swollen—he obviously couldn't be ridden.

May put her arms around his neck. "I'm sorry I've been so busy."

Macaroni stuck his nose into her hair and nickered. She rubbed her cheek against his soft coat. "I love you, Mac."

She stood back so that she could smooth Macaroni's forelock, which he especially liked. It seemed to her that his brown eyes were sad.

May felt terrible. Was Macaroni jealous of Zeus?

"I love you best, Mac," she said.

He still looked sad. May had a horrible thought: Maybe he was right to be jealous. She had been enjoying Zeus. In fact, she'd been enjoying him so much she had almost forgotten about Macaroni's sore foot.

May went back to the house, feeling terrible. She poked at her food during dinner. As soon as the meal was over, she went upstairs and got out her diary.

She wrote:

Dear Diary,

Macaroni and Zeus are both great. But they're different. Macaroni is gentle.

Zeus is adventurous. Macaroni is loyal. Zeus is smart.

May looked at what she'd just written. She felt confused. She decided to make a list.

MACARONI
Gentle
Loyal
Patient
Reliable
Neat

ZEUS
Intelligent
Adventurous
Good sense of humor
Independent
Brave

May sat back to read what she had written and was shocked. Macaroni came out sounding like a total nothing.

She had meant to highlight the differences between the two ponies. She had meant to point out that each pony was wonderful in his own way.

But was that true? When she rode Zeus, she could imagine galloping across a windswept meadow, or crossing a wild, rolling stream.

When she rode Macaroni, she usually thought about warm, comfortable things. Like Mrs. James's cookies.

Could Macaroni be dull?

7 The Terrible Truth?

As May rode Zeus the next morning, she felt guilty. She couldn't stop thinking about her diary. Her list made Macaroni sound like a bore.

Macaroni was not a bore.

On the other hand, maybe she and Macaroni weren't meant for each other. She knew that this happened sometimes. At Pine Hollow Stables, Max Regnery often talked about how important it was to match pony and rider. Sometimes, according to Max, they just didn't fit. Then it was necessary to find a new combination.

Her first pony, Luna, had been kind of poky. It had been a relief to move from Luna to Macaroni. Maybe now it was time to move from Macaroni to a pony like Zeus.

No way, May thought. She loved Macaroni, and she would love him forever.

She wished she could talk it over with Corey and Jasmine. But they were never around anymore. It was as if the two of them had disappeared from her life.

May looked up at Jasmine's bedroom window. Corey and Jasmine were probably sewing on buttons or yarn right this minute. And they didn't need May's help.

Looking at Jasmine's window made May feel sad. She turned Zeus's head and rode toward the other side of the paddock.

* * *

"We'll never finish in time," Corey groaned as she stuffed the leg of a pony pillow. She brushed her black bangs out of her eyes.

"We have to," said Jasmine grimly as she sewed eyes on the pony that had been made from her old party dress. "Mom is counting on us." She wrapped the thread around the button, pulled the thread, and snapped it.

The button fell off.

"I can't even sew," Jasmine moaned. She picked up the pony pillow. Someday it would be beautiful—if she ever finished it.

"I'm incredibly slow," Corey said as she stuffed the leg. Mrs. James had showed her how to use a crochet hook to push in the stuffing, but it was tricky. If Corey pushed too hard, the leg became stiff. If she pushed too gently, the leg stayed as limp as a noodle.

Corey's back ached. Her head ached. "How much time have we got?" she asked.

Jasmine looked at the clock over her desk. "Seven hours and twenty minutes."

"We'll never make it."

"Yes, we will," Jasmine said firmly. "But it's going to be close."

"I'll be glad when we're done," said Corey with a sigh.

"Me too," said Jasmine. "Twenty-four pony pillows is a lot."

"Sam probably doesn't even remember who I am," Corey said.

"Outlaw probably thinks I deserted him," Jasmine said.

"I miss May," said Corey. "We haven't talked to her in ages."

Corey put down the pillow. "First it was

Macaroni's foot. Then it was Zeus. I know May loves ponies, but she never seems to have time for us. Sometimes I feel like she's avoiding us."

"No way," Jasmine said.

But Corey couldn't get rid of the feeling that something was wrong. She got up from the bed and walked over to the window.

Down in the paddock May was sitting on Zeus looking up at the window.

Corey raised her hand, but May must not have seen her. May turned Zeus's head and walked him toward the other end of the paddock.

Corey opened the window and called, "May!"

But May was too far away. She didn't hear.

Corey turned back to Jasmine. "I have the feeling that May misses us as much as we miss her. A second ago she was looking up at your window."

Jasmine got up and went over to look.

At the far end of the paddock May and Zeus seemed small and lonely.

"I really miss her," Jasmine said.

Corey looked back at the bed, which was

littered with pony pillows. She remembered now that May had tried to talk her and Jasmine out of doing a sewing project.

"She didn't want us to sew," Corey said. "We weren't listening."

Jasmine nodded. "We could have picked something she liked."

"Remember when we didn't stay to watch her give Zeus a lesson?"

"We ran off," said Jasmine.

"At class on Wednesday we didn't talk about anything but pillows," Corey said.

"Some friends we are," Jasmine said.

"We don't even know if she's coming to the fair tonight," Jasmine said.

"What are we going to do?" Corey said. "The Pony Tails are supposed to solve problems. But this one is tough."

Suddenly Jasmine started to smile.

Corey wondered how Jasmine could smile at a moment like this.

"I've got a great idea," Jasmine said. "And I think it's going to work."

8 The Gift

May was grooming Zeus when she heard a sound.

"May?" said Jasmine's voice.

May felt a sudden spurt of happiness. Jasmine and Corey hadn't forgotten her after all. But then she realized that they'd probably come to talk about their craft project and how many pony pillows they'd finished.

"What?" said May, realizing that she sounded grumpy.

"Can you come out a second?" asked Corey's voice.

"Well, okay," May said.

She finished grooming Macaroni. She put the rubbing cloth back in the grooming carrier and picked the carrier up.

"See you, Mac," she said, putting her hand on his neck. These days even grooming Macaroni wasn't fun because it made her think about the entry in her diary.

She let herself out the stall door.

Corey and Jasmine were staring at her, grinning.

What is there to grin about? May wondered.

She noticed that Jasmine was holding something behind her back.

"We have something for you," Jasmine said.

It was probably something dumb, May thought. Like a spool of thread.

"Let me get rid of the grooming carrier," she said. She trudged to the tack room and put down the carrier.

She walked back. Zeus, hearing her, nickered and poked his head over his stall door. What was he feeling so good about?

Corey and Jasmine's grins were bigger than ever.

"We want you to have this," said Jasmine. From behind her back she pulled a pony pillow. It had purple button eyes and a purple yarn mane and tail. But there was something familiar about it.

"It's beautiful," May said as she reached for it. "You two are really good."

Jasmine and Corey beamed.

Suddenly May knew what was familiar about that pillow. "Your dress," she gasped. "Your favorite dress." She looked at the checked fabric with pony appliqués. "I remember when your mother made it for you." She hugged the pony to her chest. "It's perfect. Every time I look at it I'll think of you guys."

"I stuffed his legs. That's why they're crooked," Corey said with a grin.

"His legs look great," May said. "They're the best legs I ever saw."

The three Pony Tails giggled. May was happy that they were laughing.

"We're Pony Tails again," said Corey. "What a relief." She hugged May. "I'm sorry we left you out of things."

"I wasn't much of a treat myself," May said. "Thinking I could lecture you two on pony training." She shook her head. "The only reason I'm a pony trainer is by accident. Zeus's owner neglected to tell Dad that Zeus was a pony."

"I was so impressed," Corey said.

"Me too," Jasmine said. "I thought you'd never want to ride with us again."

"It's just me and my big mouth," May said. "I talked Dad into giving me a chance. And he was desperate, so he let me."

"Are you coming to the craft fair tonight?" asked Jasmine eagerly.

"You couldn't stop me," May said. Actually she was not enthusiastic about going to the fair. A gym full of crafts wasn't her idea of excitement. But it would be fun to be with Corey and Jasmine.

"Can you be ready at four?" Jasmine said. "We've got to set up. We're going to make the booth look neat."

"As in neat and tidy?" May asked gloomily.

"You don't have to do anything," Corey said. "You can supervise."

Suddenly May burst out laughing.

"What?" Corey and Jasmine asked at the same time.

"I've been thinking I had a terrible problem," May said, "but now I realize it's not a problem. I got so excited about Zeus that I began to think Macaroni wasn't for me.

Macaroni is sensible and levelheaded. You might say he's my exact opposite."

"So?" said Jasmine and Corey.

May took a deep breath. She knew she had to tell them about the list she'd made in her diary. She felt terrible about the list, but she had to be honest. "I made this comparison of Zeus and Macaroni in my diary, and Macaroni came out looking like a total creep."

"He's not!" Corey said. "He's the greatest."

"Of course he is," May said. "He's just different. And that's the whole point. One of the things that Mac and I love about each other is that we're different."

"Like me and Sam," said Corey.

"And me and Outlaw," said Jasmine.

"And like the Pony Tails," May said. "One of the things that makes us crazy about each other is that we're totally different."

"Except for being pony-crazy," Corey said.

"Anyway, I'll treasure this pillow all my life," May said, hugging it.

"Which reminds me," Jasmine said.

"What?" asked May.

"We have a dozen pony pillows to finish in the next six hours."

"A dozen?" said May, her face filling with horror.

"We can do it if we work together," Jasmine said.

"I'll help," May said. "Even if I sew the eyes on backward and the tails on upside down. But first I have an important mission. I have to see my best friend."

"I thought we were your best friends," Corey said.

"My best pony friend," May said. "Macaroni."

"Take your time," said Jasmine as she and Corey headed back to the house.

May went into the feed room. She got the cardboard box that was filled with carrots and looked for exactly the right one. It couldn't be yellow and woody. It couldn't be too big because Macaroni was a pony. Finally she found one that was small and orange and crisp.

When she entered Macaroni's stall, he looked at her with sad brown eyes.

May felt terrible. Until this moment she hadn't really understood how upset Macaroni was.

"I have to tell you something," May said. "I'm a complete jerk."

Macaroni nuzzled her elbow. It was nice to see that he didn't agree.

"I am, though," May said. "It's just that there was so much going on: your corn, the new pony, and the craft fair. I almost forgot about you. I never will again."

May held out the carrot. Macaroni sniffed it and looked it over. It wasn't his way to be greedy. He nibbled the end and then bit off a chunk.

"We may be opposites, but that doesn't mean we can't love each other," May said.

Macaroni nickered. For a second May thought he was agreeing with her, but then she realized he wanted the other half of the carrot.

Macaroni finished chewing the carrot and swallowed it. His head was up now. His eyes were shiny.

May headed for the stall door. "Hold on, Mac," May said. "You are about to get the superdeluxe grooming of your life."

9 At the Craft Fair

At four o'clock that afternoon the Pony Tails and Mrs. James piled into the Jameses' car.

"How are you feeling, Mrs. J.?" asked May.

"Much better," Mrs. James said, "especially since you girls made all those pillows."

As Mrs. James started the car, May said, "Do you think the new baby will like ponies?"

Mrs. James smiled. "It's hard to tell."

"My mother loves horses, my father loves horses, but my two sisters couldn't care less," May said. "It's really strange. Why does it turn out that way?"

"I don't think anybody knows," Mrs. James said.

"We could hang pictures of ponies near the baby's crib so she'll be pony-conscious right from the start," said Corey.

"It couldn't hurt," Mrs. James said.

"And we could get pony baby books," said May.

"That's definitely a good idea," Mrs. James said. "I can tell this baby is going to have a good time."

* * *

The craft fair was being held in the gym of Willow Creek Elementary School, so the Pony Tails knew their way around.

Jasmine carried the bag of pony pillows, while Corey and May helped Mrs. James carry the tea cozies, place mats, and clothes-pin dolls she had made.

With the booths set up, the gym looked entirely different.

"Just think, a month from now we'll be back here," May said glumly.

"So let's enjoy ourselves while we can," Corey said.

May Rides a New Pony

Mrs. James's booth was under the basketball hoop at the far end of the gym. The fair organizers had supplied her with a table and a bookcase.

"Hmmm," May said, standing back. "The way you display items is very important." May hadn't been interested in making the pony pillows, but selling them was something else.

May eyed the table and bookcase. "I would suggest an exciting row of pony pillows marching across the center of the table."

"Good idea," said Mrs. James.

Jasmine emptied the bag of pony pillows onto the table, and she and Corey arranged them into a long row.

"You shouldn't put everything out at once," May said. "It's too crowded." She arranged ten ponies in a circle as if they were chasing each other. "I think the tea cozies would look nice along the back," she said.

Mrs. James arranged the cozies in a row. They looked like small, colorful hills behind the ponies.

"And I think the clothespin dolls would look nice on both sides," May said. Mrs.

James made the world's greatest clothespin dolls. May had a whole family of them at home. They lived in her dollhouse.

May stood back. "It's getting better."

Jasmine and Corey nodded. The table looked colorful and interesting.

"We could put the place mat sets on the shelves," May said. She looked at Jasmine. "You could arrange them artistically."

Jasmine arranged the place mats in a fan shape.

"Great," May said. "We're going to make a million, and the fair is going to make a zillion."

"I think we're all set," Mrs. James said. "Why don't you girls have a look around before the public is admitted?"

It was a large fair. May had to admit that some of the crafts were interesting. There was a booth full of macramé jewelry made of string.

"How do you do that?" Jasmine said, peering at a necklace that was as fine as a spider's web.

"Very slowly," said the woman behind the table with a smile and a wink.

"I bet," Corey said.

The next booth was filled with ceramic jewelry.

"We could do that," Jasmine said. "My mother has a kiln."

"Er . . . ," May said.

Jasmine clapped her hand to her forehead. "Sorry, no more craft projects for a while."

"Thank you," May said.

The next table was filled with cornhusk dolls. May knew that long ago, when people couldn't afford to buy regular dolls, they made cornhusk dolls for their children. The dolls were nice, May thought, but if she were a little kid, she would prefer one with hair.

The next booth had a horse theme. There were horse neckties, horse belts, and horse scarves. May looked at a red necktie with horses' heads printed on it. "I could get this for my father for Christmas," she said. "It's Christmassy."

"And horsey," Corey said.

May turned it over to look for the price. A small white tag read $20.

"Twenty dollars!" May said.

"It's real silk," said the man at the booth.

"It's really nice," May said, "but I don't think I can afford it."

"We have a horse key chain that costs less," the man said.

May thought of her father's keys. With the barn, the feed room, the tack room, the house, the horse trailer, and the station wagon, Mr. Grover had about a hundred keys.

"He's got so many keys he has to keep them on a metal ring," May said.

"Oh well," said the man with a smile.

"Will you look at that!" Corey said.

The next booth was filled with things for horses. There were beautiful handwoven saddle blankets, and rosettes for decorating bridles. On the left was a rack with spools and spools of ribbon to braid into a horse's mane and tail.

"Not bad," May said, stepping close. There was something about the shininess of the ribbons that made her think of Macaroni.

"Which color is best for Mac?" she asked Corey and Jasmine.

"Brown would go well with his yellow coat," Corey said.

May shook her head. "Brown is good. But I want something more exciting."

"How about red?" asked Jasmine. She knew that red was one of May's favorite colors.

May thought a minute. "Too hot."

"Plaid?" asked Corey.

"Too fussy," said May.

"Stripes?" asked Jasmine.

"Too stripey."

Corey looked at Jasmine. "I think May has something in mind."

"Green," said May. She lifted the end of the green ribbon and let it slip through her fingers. Right away Jasmine could see that May was right. The green would look perfect braided into Macaroni's mane.

"I want to decorate a pony's mane," May said to the woman who was minding the booth. "How much ribbon do I need?"

"Is it a big pony or a small pony?" the woman asked.

May thought a minute. "Medium."

"Then I would advise three yards."

May reached into her pocket and got her wallet. Her dad had given her money to spend at the fair. "I'll take it."

The woman measured the ribbon against a yardstick that had been taped to the back of the table. She cut off three yards.

"Your pony will enjoy that," she said with a smile.

"He deserves it," May said. "He's been having a hard time."

"I'm sorry to hear that," the woman said politely.

All at once there was a rush of fresh air and the sound of many voices talking at the same time.

"The fair has opened," Jasmine said. "Back to the booth."

The girls dashed back.

"There are hundreds of people here," May said as she watched the aisles grow crowded. "We're bound to sell out in a matter of minutes."

A woman stopped to look at the pony pillows. "Those are very nice," she said.

"Thanks," said Corey, Jasmine, and May together.

"Did you make them yourselves?" the woman asked.

"Totally," Jasmine said.

"They're very neatly done," the woman said. She smiled and walked away.

"And I thought for sure we had a sale," May said.

A man came up and said, "Those are interesting pillows."

"Thanks," Corey said. "We made them ourselves."

"Nice work," he said. "You should be proud of yourselves."

He walked away.

A woman came up and bought two of Mrs. James's tea cozies. "These will make wonderful Christmas presents," she said. The Pony Tails watched jealously as Mrs. James wrapped the two cozies and took the woman's money.

"I bet we don't sell a single pillow," said Corey miserably. "All that work for nothing."

"I guess the pillows are sloppy," Jasmine said.

"Not at all," said Mrs. James.

"Then how come no one is buying them?" Jasmine asked.

"They're lovely pillows. That's what counts," Mrs. James said.

Ha! thought May. What counts is how many pillows we sell.

A woman in a blue blouse drifted past the booth.

"Excuse me, ma'am," May said. "But I can't help noticing your beautiful blue blouse."

"Why, thank you," the woman said, looking down at it. "It's my favorite color."

"I must say it flatters you," May said.

"It does?" The woman smiled with pleasure.

"Blue is a color you can never afford to do without," May said. "For that reason you can't afford to pass up this one-of-a-kind blue pony pillow." She held up a blue pony with a blue mane and a blue tail. "Note his stunning tail. Have you ever seen such a fabulous shade of blue? Note his sparkling blue eyes. If I might say so"—May took a deep breath—"this is the pony pillow of a lifetime. If you pass it up, you'll never find another half so good."

May thrust the pillow into the woman's hands.

The woman examined the pillow. "It is cute," she said.

"*Cute* hardly describes it," May said. "It's dazzling, it's dynamic, it's dashing." She pointed to the pillow. "This pillow says something about you."

"I have a granddaughter who loves horses," the woman said.

"What more can I say?" May said. "I bet she loves blue just like you."

"As a matter of fact, she does," said the woman with a smile.

"Congratulations, you've just made the best decision of your life," said May.

Before the woman knew what was happening, she had paid for the pillow and carried it away.

"Do tea cozies really work?" said a man with a gray mustache to Mrs. James. "I've always wondered."

"Work?" May said. "These cozies work so well they're positively dangerous. Your tea won't be hot. It will be scorching."

"I hate lukewarm tea," the man said.

"Okay, picture this," May said. "You're getting ready to watch your favorite TV show."

The man nodded.

"You want tea," May said. "But what do

CRAFT FAIR
PONY

you fear and dread? Lukewarm tea. So what do you do? You take the teapot into your TV room. You cover the pot with the cozy. Throughout the show you will have piping-hot tea."

"Who could resist?" the man said. He looked along the line of cozies, trying to select one.

"For a man of your distinction I suggest this one," said May, pointing to a black, white, and red cozy. And to go with it I suggest this tasteful pony pillow." She held up a pillow that was black, white, and red.

"Er, what would I do with that?" the man said.

"Put it in the chair next to you," May said. "That way you will never be lonely."

The man smiled. "I see what you mean. Those long winter nights can be lonesome."

"Your life will never lack companionship again," May said. Before the man was quite sure what had happened, he had paid for the cozy and the pillow.

As he walked away, Mrs. James said, "May, you're amazing."

"That's her," said Jasmine proudly. "May the Amazing."

"You could sell anything," said Corey.

"Excuse me," said a girl about their age. "Is this where I can buy those pony pillows?"

"The very place itself," May said, "but they're going fast. If I were you, I'd make my selection right away."

Carefully the girl examined each pony pillow. She was obviously having trouble making up her mind.

"These pillows make ideal presents," May said. "If you have friends who like ponies, these pillows will make them eternally happy."

"Do you think so?" the girl asked.

"I know so," May said. "I just got a pony pillow and it was the best gift I ever received."

Corey and Jasmine beamed.

The girl picked out three pillows and said, "Can you hold them for me while I get my mother?"

"No problem," said May grandly. "These pillows are on reserve."

Mr. James had come to join them in the booth. He was an ecologist, and usually he was quiet and thoughtful, but now he was laughing. "You're great, May. You're the best salesperson I ever saw."

Jasmine and Corey looked at each other. Who would have imagined that May's talent for talking to people would come in so handy?

The girl came back with her mother.

"They're really lovely," her mother said. "You're absolutely right."

"She has a good eye," May said.

The mother beamed.

May leaned forward and whispered loudly to the girl, "You look like a nice girl."

The girl blinked.

"I bet you have a lot of friends," May said.

The girl nodded.

"To spare them heartbreak, warn them that these pony pillows are almost gone."

10 Best Friends Forever

"I can't believe it," said May, flopping into a chair at the booth. It was the first time she'd sat down all evening. "We sold every pillow."

Jasmine and Corey flopped into chairs on either side.

"We could have sold a hundred," said May enthusiastically. "Too bad you guys didn't make more."

Corey and Jasmine looked at each other and groaned.

"Thanks to you, May, all my things are sold," Mrs. James said. She looked at the empty table and the empty shelves. "I can't believe it."

"We've got the only booth that sold out completely," said Jasmine proudly.

"I wonder how everyone else at the fair did," Mr. James said. "It looks like it was a good night."

The Pony Tails looked around. None of the other booths had sold out, but they had sold a lot.

"Good evening," said a booming voice over the loudspeaker. "We are proud to announce that this year's craft fair made fifty percent more than last year."

There was a round of applause. The people who had been working at the booths looked proud.

"The fair did so well that it exceeded its goals."

"They made more money than they hoped?" May said. "That's amazing."

"Not only will Willow Creek Elementary School be able to buy computers for the library, but there will be money left over."

A gasp ran through the gym.

"So we'll have ice cream for lunch every day," May said. "And cookies. And chocolate cake."

"The PTA has decided to donate the extra money to the Belleville Elementary School library so that it can buy computers too."

"That's even better," said May.

The exhibitors began to pack up.

Mrs. James and the Pony Tails had nothing to pack up because everything had been sold.

"Come on, girls," Mr. James said. "You must be tired. Let's go home."

* * *

When they arrived at the Jameses' house, May yawned and said, "It's been a long day, but I have to do one more thing."

"What?" said Jasmine.

"Say good-night to Mac," May said.

"We'll keep you company," said Corey.

They followed the Pony Trail through Jasmine's backyard into Corey's and then into May's. It was almost dark now. Wind was blowing up from the Silverado River.

"I figured out something about friendship," May said as they walked into the Grovers' barn.

"What's that?" Jasmine said.

"It's like riding," May said. "It's easy to take it for granted and stop paying attention."

"When you forget to pay attention, everything goes wrong," Corey said.

They walked toward Macaroni's stall. When he heard them, he turned and nickered.

"He's not asleep," May said. "Let's go in and say good-night." They walked to the front of Macaroni's stall.

"If I had paid more attention to Macaroni, he wouldn't have gotten jealous of Zeus," May said. She reached out and rubbed Macaroni's yellow nose. "I'm sorry, Mac."

"If Corey and I hadn't gotten so wound up in the craft project, you wouldn't have felt left out," said Jasmine.

"It's okay," May said. "I think we all learned something."

Jasmine tickled Macaroni under his forelock. "Some week, huh, Mac? First you get a corn and then you're totally ignored."

"He doesn't look so miserable," Corey said. "In fact, he looks pretty happy."

"I almost forgot!" May said. Out of her pocket she pulled a bag. Out of the bag she pulled three yards of green ribbon. She held it up to Macaroni's yellow mane.

"It's perfect," Jasmine said. "You can

save it for the next big event at Pine Hollow."

"Totally," May said. She dangled the ribbon in front of Macaroni. "What do you think of that?"

Macaroni sniffed the ribbon and nudged it with his nose. When he figured out that it wasn't edible, he lost interest and nuzzled May's ear.

"You'll like the ribbon when I braid it in your hair," May said. She knew Macaroni loved to look fancy.

"I guess he hasn't had such a bad week after all," Corey said.

They bent over to examine his right foot. The special shoe that the blacksmith had put on it was strange-looking. But the foot looked much better.

"The blacksmith is coming on Monday to check his foot," May said. "Pretty soon he'll be back to normal."

The girls filed out of Macaroni's stall into the aisle. Overhead a lightbulb inside a metal guard sent out warm yellow light.

Jasmine yawned. "I'm going to dream of pillows, that's for sure."

Corey giggled. "I'm going to dream about May's sales talk."

"Wait a second," May said sternly. "Aren't we forgetting something?"

"What?" asked Jasmine, rubbing her eyes.

"We were talking about not taking things for granted."

Sleepily, Corey and Jasmine nodded.

"We were talking about paying attention to people and ponies."

"So?" said Corey. "I don't get it."

"What about Zeus?" May said. "He's going to be living here all month. He has feelings, too."

"There's so much to remember," Corey groaned. "Sometimes I feel like my head is going to pop."

From the other end of the barn came the sound of nickering and prancing. It was a light sound, a frisky sound. It couldn't be anyone but Zeus.

"To think we nearly forgot him," Corey wailed. "The poor thing."

They walked to Zeus's stall. He was pawing at the bedding. He bobbed his head up and down to show that he was glad to see them.

May opened the stall door. "Hi, Zeus," she

said, walking in. Jasmine and Corey followed her. Zeus watched them with his bright, friendly eyes.

"I'm really glad you're staying with us," May said, stroking his soft nose.

"Me too," Jasmine said. She reached out and tickled the spot between Zeus's ears. "I haven't gotten to know you very well because I've been busy. But I know we're going to like each other. You know something else? You're going to like Outlaw, and he's going to like you." She smiled. "But I have to warn you, he can be a real handful sometimes."

Zeus looked at her gravely.

"If you hear weird sounds in the night, it's just my dog, Dracula," Corey said. "Or if you think you hear a car screeching, it's my parrot, Bluebeard."

"Except for Corey's pets, she's totally normal," May said to Zeus.

"And I know you and my pony, Sam, will really like each other," Corey said.

Zeus frisked from one foot to another as if he couldn't wait for the night to be over and a new day to begin.

"I've got something for you," May said.

With a flourish she pulled a bag from her left pocket. Out of it she pulled a yellow ribbon. "How do you think this would look in his mane?" she asked.

"Great," Jasmine said. "But where did you get it?"

"I remembered that I'd forgotten Zeus," May said, "so I went back to the booth and bought it."

"Good thinking," Corey said.

"For once I was paying attention." May put her hand on Zeus's neck. "Even though Macaroni will always be number one, I love you both. When you go home to the Randalls at the end of the month, you're going to go in style."

"Maybe we could help you train him," said Corey shyly. "I know you know a lot more than we do, but we could learn."

"I don't know anything," May said. "I need all the help I can get."

"You're not just saying that?" said Jasmine.

"No way," May said. "We'll train Zeus together. It'll be fun."

Jasmine sighed. "You know what? The summer seems pretty perfect now that the Pony Tails are a team again."

When May got home, she took out her diary and wrote:

Dear Diary,

Today was the best day of my life. I would tell you all about it, but I am totally, totally pooped. Tomorrow I'll tell you everything.

May slipped the diary under her pillow. She put the special pony pillow on top of it. Then she lay down and fell asleep, and she dreamed about ponies.

May's Pony Training Tips

I love the fact that my father trains horses for a living. If you don't count my two sisters (and I usually don't), everybody in my family *loves* to talk about horses. It's the next best thing to riding them (and hugging them).

It was a lot of fun to work with Dad on schooling Zeus. I learned a lot about training in general and an awful lot about training Zeus in particular.

There are two things you always have to do when you're training a pony. First, you have to repeat the same lessons over and over until the pony gets the idea. I ride Macaroni almost every day, and when I'm training him we go over a lot of the same basic things each time. Mac has learned to stand still when I mount him; to walk, trot, canter, and jump on command; and to step into the trailer like a gentleman.

The second thing, and it's really part of the first thing, is that you have to be consistent. That means that the way you ask your pony to do something has to be the same every time. For instance, when I taught Zeus to walk faster without breaking into a trot, I gave little squeezes on his belly with the rhythm of his walk, and I loosened the reins a bit. I always asked that way because if I had done something else—like tapping him with my riding crop—then he might have thought I wanted him to do something different, like break into a trot.

The great thing is that ponies are smart. Lucky for me, Macaroni's not *just* smart—he always wants to please me, so he really tries to understand what I'm telling him to do. Once he understands, he may need some reminders, but he'll do it right most of the time—until eventually he does it right all the time. That's why it pays to repeat an exercise—and to make sure you give consistent instructions—until your pony understands what you want.

Trainers use a lot of different aids to work

with ponies and horses, but the two most common are a longe line and cavalletti.

A longe (pronounce it as if it were spelled *lunge*) is like a long leash, attached to a special bridle. The trainer stands in the middle of the ring, and the pony goes in a circle around her. When I have Macaroni on a longe line, I use a very long whip. It's long so that it can reach the pony, but it's not meant to hurt—just to get attention! When a pony is on a longe line, the trainer can see things she might never notice if she were riding the pony, like the way the pony holds his neck. It also helps the pony learn to move at a steady pace.

When I first began training Macaroni to jump, I used cavalletti, or ground poles. (*Cavalletti* is an Italian word, and it refers to two or more poles. If there is only one pole, it's called a cavalletto.) Those are long rails that are laid on the ground for the pony to step over. Once Macaroni and I were comfortable going over the ground poles, Dad and I began putting the poles on supports that hold them a few inches off the ground. Every time we went over the cavalletti, I leaned forward a bit and lifted myself out of the saddle and moved my hands forward to loosen the reins, even when we were just walking and Macaroni was just stepping over the pole. You probably know that's called jump position. We weren't really jumping, but it was a way of being consistent because we were *going to* jump.

Then Dad raised the cavalletti, and *bingo,* Macaroni couldn't just step over the cavalletti, so he jumped. Macaroni's first jump was easy—and *wonderful.* Since we'd been repeating the same actions again and again and we were being consistent, it was a breeze for both of us. When Dad helped us, I'm not sure whether he was actually training Macaroni or me. I don't think it matters, though. We both learned, didn't we?

Cavalletti can also be used to work on a pony's gaits. For example, if you want to train your pony to have a longer stride, you can lay a course of poles for him to step over that makes him take bigger steps. If you repeat the course enough and if you're consistent in your signals, he'll get the idea. However, you'll need help in deciding exactly how far apart the poles should be. The ideal stride length is different for different ponies.

It took my dad years and years to become

a trainer. He says that every time he works with a new horse or pony, he learns something new. He also says good training is based on trust and understanding and that the only way to achieve that is to be consistent so that the horse knows he can trust you.

The other thing Dad always says is that he wishes I were as easy to train as a horse. I wonder what he means by *that*!

About the Author

Bonnie Bryant was born and raised in New York City, and she still lives there today. She spends her summers in a house on a lake in Massachusetts.

Ms. Bryant began writing about girls and horses when she started The Saddle Club in 1987. So far there are more than sixty books in that series. Much as she likes telling the stories about Stevie, Carole, and Lisa, she decided that the younger riders at Pine Hollow Stables, especially May Grover, have stories of their own that need telling. That's how Pony Tails was born.

Ms. Bryant rides horses when she has time away from her computer, but she doesn't have a horse of her own. She likes to ride different horses and enjoys a variety of riding experiences. She says she thinks most of her readers are much better riders than she is!